ROTHERHAM LIBRARY & INFORMATION SERVICES

This book must be returned by the date specified at the time of issue
as the DATE DUE FOR RETURN.
The loan may be extended (personally, by post or telephone) for a
further period if the book is not required by another reader, by quoting
the above number / author / title.

LIS7a

For Sophie

First published 1990 by
Walker Books Ltd, 87 Vauxhall Walk
London SE11 5HJ

This edition published 1999

2 4 6 8 10 9 7 5 3 1

© 1990 Philippe Dupasquier

Printed in Hong Kong/China

British Library Cataloguing in Publication Data
A catalogue record for this book is
available from the British Library.

ISBN 0-7445-6944-3

I CAN'T SLEEP

PHILIPPE DUPASQUIER

WALKER BOOKS
AND SUBSIDIARIES
LONDON • BOSTON • SYDNEY

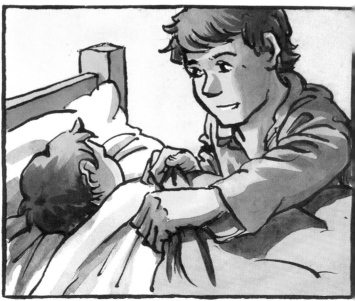

MORE WALKER PAPERBACKS
For You to Enjoy

Also by Philippe Dupasquier

FOLLOW THAT CHIMP

When Chimp escapes from the zoo, his keepers follow him, and the
most amazing pursuit begins – across land, sea and air; on trains, planes, cars and ships…
But will Chimp get away? Follow his adventures in this action-packed comic-strip picture book.

"A prolonged, hectic, hilarious chase." *Books for Keeps*

0-7445-2511-X   £3.99

THE GREAT ESCAPE

A prisoner is chased by a gang of warders in this classic wordless picture book.

"Brilliant and breathless… Each scene is packed with comic detail."
The Times Literary Supplement

0-7445-4714-8   £4.99